Love Me Now

A Short Valentine Story

Bethel-Gold

Ukiyoto Publishing

All global publishing rights are held by

Ukiyoto Publishing

Published in 2022

ISBN 9789356450233

Thankful to GOD, my mum, siblings and everyone who supported me through my journey.

Contents

1

The Breakup

The bell rang and she groaned then buried her face further into her couch pillow with the hope that whoever was ringing the bell would get tired and stop so she can continue her heavyweight crying.

The ringing persisted and she sat up and stayed put to wait if the person would stop and leave.

When she heard no ringing, she lay back on the floor and used the duvet she dragged from her bedroom to cover her entire petite frame.

Ding dong!

It sounded again and more groans of anger and sadness left her.

First, it was her ex texting her about canceling on the trip and breaking it off with her because he didn't see a future with her anymore, now someone was violently ringing her doorbell.

The thought of getting rid of that annoying bell switch so as to reduce pain and disturbance for her went through her mind and she thought it was great not until the image of people knocking on her door because they wanted to see her went past her mind and she decided the bell was better and more civil.

So, she removed the duvet from her body and stood up to go check who had decided to disturb her when she was at her weakest.

Then it occurred to her that her sisters must have heard and sent their number one amebo a.k.a 'I see and I exaggerate' Funmi.
She looked a mess and if she saw her in this way, then she would go and tell the remaining gangs and they will know how bad she is affected by the breakup and would continue to torment her that she can't keep a relationship that isn't about business.
She didn't even have the strength to go look good for anyone and made up her mind not to put to mind whatever they might throw at her.
Those words might not count since she will be too busy nursing a broken heart.
Packing her braided hair in a ponytail, she got closer to the door and yanked it open.
"If you are here to mo-" she stopped mid-sentence when she saw her two great twin friends, Dara and Dora standing in front of her domot both with smiles embracing their faces but it died when they saw how she looked.
"What is going on Ife?" Dora asked going to engulf her in a hug while Dara walked in with the wine-colored bag she was holding in both hands.
They closed the door behind them and locked it before walking her to the small crying temple she created.
"Why are you crying?" Dara asked coming to sit beside her while caressing her head.
"I thought you guys heard already"
"Heard what?" Dora asked still allowing her to rest on her shoulder.

She raised her head from resting on Dara's shoulder to look at both sisters before a sob escaped from her lips and she placed her hand over her mouth to conceal the sobs that kept coming.
"Tomiwa ended us... over a text message. A text message D's" she called them the nickname she uses when she wants to call them at the same time.
"Oh my GOD," Dara said just at the same time Dora said.
"What?"
"Yes, it's all ended. All finished, my heart is broken, my world has ended" Ife cried.
"No, no don't say that Ifeoluwa. This isn't the end of you or your world" Dara consoled.
"Yes, it is, like how would I do this? Two years, D's two good years, and six months of being engaged it all ended with a text message. Ah, óti parí fún mi báyì" Ife cried.
"Eh, eh don't talk like that Ife, this isn't the end of time. Just because he cowardly ended things doesn't mean it is over for you." Dara said.
"Maybe he isn't the right one for you sef. Even I have been saying that guy has no good intention from the beginning" Dora muttered the last part and her twin threw her a glare to caution what she was saying.
"Don't mind Dora, look at the bright side at least you were not married when he decided to end things"
"Is it not the same thing? After all that I have done for that man, this is what he chose to pay me back with, ah Tomiwa, olórun yíò dárí jìné"

"Like, I had everything laid out for our trip to Maldives, we were supposed to spend next week there since it is valentine's week, how then will I do it? Face the shame and insult my sisters will be ready to throw at me? How?" she cried.

"Don't put them in mind, you don't want to put too much pressure on yourself all because of this breakup."

"I am going to be a laughing stock for all my family after they are aware of it, chai. This life eh" she ignored what they were saying and continued her lamenting.

"Did he give a meaningful reason as to why he was breaking up with you?" Dora asked opening one of the bags they brought.

Ife stood up to go and pick up her phone then scrolled to the message she got from him early in the morning.

Dara collected the phone and read it out loud.

"Ifeoluwa, I am sorry but I will have to cancel that trip you made for us to that place and just so you know, the wedding is off. Nothing between us, we are done, no engagement or anything. Hope you heal properly and have a nice day, wink emoji" she put the phone down and looked at her twin sister who shook her head.

"He better be joking," Dara said after a while of recovering from the shock she got when she read the message.

"That boy na werey him be. Shey na so dem dey end relationship? That guy no well at all" Dora said angrily and handed Ifeoluwa a plate of fried rice and chicken.
"See, food is not what is doing me at the moment," Ife said turning down the food.
"Eh, I bet you didn't have anything to eat yesterday since you are a light eater and with this message, you will not want to eat. You better eat something and not let a man that doesn't care about how you are feeling make you sick" Dora said.
"Is there enough ponmo and ẹ□dọ□ there?" she asked eyeing the plate of rice from her side.
"Just like you love it" she assured her and Ife took it then began digging into the food.
"Let's forget about that boy, if he doesn't need you, you definitely don't need him at all, and as for dealing with your sisters when you meet. Just ignore them, people who have nothing to do with their lives tend to poke their smelling noses in other people's affairs, all will be good" Dora told her and she nod her head.
"How about the trip? Do I cancel it?" she asked them.
"Hmm..." both sisters said at the same time.
"Why don't you find someone to go with you?" Dara suggested.
"Like a male friend," Dora piped in.
"Why male?" Ife frowned and looked in between them.
"No, don't get it the wrong way. He will go as a friend"
"Yeah, just a friendly travel and you could use that time to clear your mind as you are away"

"Remind me why you both can't come?"
"We have a show to run and on the eve of valentine and the day of valentine will be the time we will spend with our partners," Dara told her and she groaned.
"I feel so alone, ow! What was that for?" she exclaimed when Dora pinched her arm.
"Now you don't feel alone anymore," she told her and she shrugged then continued eating.
"Do you feel better now?" Dara asked also taking a plate of assorted egusi soup and eba after she went to wash her hands in the kitchen.
Dora took a plate of Jollof rice and began eating.
"Yeah, I feel a bit better"
"Bit ke? I know say no be heartbreak dey do you like that. Na because say you dey hungry, na why d tin hit you hard" Dora said to lighten the mood and Ife hissed then looked at Dara's plate of food.
"Why didn't you bring egusi for me too?"
"Kini? Shebi na fried rice wey dey your front like that? Why you con dey look my side?" she turned away from her so she can eat properly without having Ifeoluwa pluck out a piece of meat from her food.
"But you know say I go like egusi soup too"
"Eh, next time. Face your food"
"Okay, oya just put small egusi for me please" she begged and Dara looked at her then put some egusi and a piece of meat which made Ife grin widely.
"Na because say you dey nurse heartbreak oo"
"Ọrẹ mi, ese" she thanked and continued eating her food.
"I love you girls," she said after a while.

"We love you too," they both said at the same time.

***

Translations

Amebo is gossip.
Domot is entrance of a house.
Óti parí fún mi báyì - my own has finished.
Olórun yíò dárí jìné - GOD will forgive you.
Chai is an exclamation.
That boy na werey him be - That boy isn't stable mentally.
Shey na so dem dey end relationship? - is that how to end a relationship?
That guy no well at all - that guy isn't in any way okay.
Ponmo is cow skin.
Ẹ□ dọ□ is liver.
Egusi soup - also known as melon soup and made from melon seed.
Eba is made from garri (cassava flakes)
Jollof rice is a popular food here in Nigeria.
Ke? - like a questioning word.
I know say no be heartbreak dey do you like that - I know it was just the heartbreak that made you that way.
Na because say you dey hungry, na why d tin hit you hard - it is because you are hungry that was why it made you hurt a lot.
Kini? - what?
Shebi na fried rice wey dey your front like that? - isn't that fried rice you have in front of you?

Why you con dey look my side? - why then are you looking at my food?
But you know say I go like egisi soup too - but you are aware I will love a plate of egusi soup too.
Oya - is like saying 'quick, quickly'. It's a persuasive word.
Na because say you dey nurse heartbreak oo - it is because you are nursing a broken heart.
Ọrẹ mi, ese - my friend, thank you.

Patrick

It has been two days since her heart-wrenching break up and instead of sulking like she originally wanted to do, she decided to go get some more sanitary pads.

It was surprising her period came too early in the month and she had just a few pieces left. Hence, her leaving the house.

The twins did make things easier for her and would call to check on her and let her know that all is well and that she will be fine.

It made her feel better that they kept sending more food her way so she didn't see any reason to cry aside from when she watched titanic the previous night.

She was a crying mess as she explained to Dara how Jack died and why he shouldn't have died and left Rose in this cruel world.

Dara was elated she slept in no time after her long crying explanation.

"No more thinking, I will be fine," she said to herself and came out of her car, locked it, and checked if it was really locked before heading into the building.

Her phone rang and she paused to take it out of her purse to see who was calling and as expected her mum was calling and she wondered how come it took this long for them to confirm whatever news they heard about her.

"Ifeoluwa Tobiloba" her mum began and she resist the urge to roll her eyes and continue her way into the feminine aisle to get what she came here for.

"Ma" she answered in a not too pleasing manner.

"Ifeoluwa Ayomipo Gra-"

"Mummy why did you call?" she interrupted her mum.

Her mum didn't have to go to that extent of calling her entire name if she was just calling to make fun of her along with the rest of her sisters.

"So, you are now cutting your mummy off abi?" her mother asked sounding annoyed but she didn't answer and just stood in front of a particular sanitary product she wanted to try on.

"You don't want to answer abi? No problem, maybe that is what you were taught in school to disrespect your parents and elders, okay ooo"

A sigh left Ife's lips as she knew this particular tactic her mum uses especially on her so even if her mum is at fault Ife would look like the bad one and her mum like the victim.

"Mummy, please I don't have time for all this drama today, I don't have energy for it. Please tell me why you called so I can get on with my day" she told her mum already feeling frustrated.

"That is why I told your dad, may his soul rest in peace, that he shouldn't allow you to go abroad to study that business thing you went to study. See how it has made you, can you see?" her mother lamented and she shook her head.

"When I said you should school here in Nigeria as your sisters did, you wouldn't be talking to your elders disrespectfully like you are doing and will be able to keep a relationship firm and even get married"

"One of your daughters who you said to have 'good culture' instilled in them got kicked out of her husband's house just because she bad-mouthed and insulted her mother-in-law" she began unable to take the insult her mum threw her way.

"The other one, 'a public property' to the entire men in our community, and I am the one with the bad values instilled" she shook her head and tried to keep the tears in.

"I wished dad never died so I wouldn't have to face all these embarrassments I am facing from you lots. You claim to be my real mother, if truly you are then act like one and stop judging me" she disconnected the call and didn't wait for whatever her mother had to say to her.

She already had enough of them and their attacking words towards her.

It wasn't her fault Tomiwa decided to leave her without a valid reason and when they had months to get married and a planned-out week in Maldives. It wasn't her fault and she wouldn't let them keep trashing her and getting away with it.

She closed her eyes to keep the tears in so she wouldn't break down and when she opened her eyes, there wasn't anyone close to her and was glad she didn't raise her voice and cause an unnecessary scene.

"Ife, you got this, no one can march you anyhow. You will be good" she told herself and looked at the pads on the shelves.

Just as she was going to grab two packs, she heard her name being called from behind and no one calls her that except one person.

"Grace? Is that you?" the voice said again and she turned around to confirm her suspicion.

It was confirmed as shock, disbelief, surprise, and amusement played on her face when she saw him.

"Patrick?" she asked to be sure and the fine dark-skinned man nodded with a grin that made his dimples pop from both cheeks.

That same flutter she felt whenever she saw his dimples came and she looked at him from his neatly styled punk hair to his face that had no trace of beard but had his dimples popping out with his handsome, head-spinning smile.

His brows were full like they had always been and were shaped with a small cut at the edge of the right brow.

He wasn't that chubby guy she used to know in college, rather he was built with his well-defined torso and biceps that could be seen from his grey t-shirt hugging them.

Was it illegal that she wanted to be that shirt?

Her eyes traveled further down to his waist that had a black belt strapping dark blue slightly tight jeans with a black pair of sneakers honoring his feet.

His dark skin is well defined and glowing.

He is the definition of gorgeous.

Who would think that the Patrick of that time, the nerdy-looking chubby but adorable looking guy would turn out to be this gorgeous-looking blank panther? Black Panther? Seriously Ife, you could do better she scolded herself.

Beautiful black king, she thought but 'black panther' suited him more in her definition.

"How are you doing?" he asked going in for a hug but she was too possessed by his look to give the hug back.

"You look good" the words just flew out of her mouth and she didn't have the chance to think about anything but just say what was in her mind.

His cheeks warmed up by the comment coming from her and he bit his bottom lip to contain the huge grin wanting to be known.

"It's great hearing that from my long-time crush," he said to her and she froze, then her eyes went wide before adjusting to their normal size when he said that.

Their story was something to talk about... Like that.

When they were in college over there in the US he had always made his intentions known to her but she saw him more as a friend and would let him know so she doesn't lead him on and break his heart.

There was a time she thought she liked him so much but didn't want anything occurring between them to be more than friendship so she avoided him for a while because she liked Tomiwa she met when came home for vacation at that time.

But it seems like the feelings are resurfacing but she thinks it is because of the massive change in his physical appearance that is making her feel this way.
"It is still there?" she asked and he nodded with a smile.
"Always" he grinned widely.
She found herself getting lost in that beautiful smile again and had to caution herself and look away to collect her thoughts that don't seem to exist anymore.
Looking back at him with a clear head and a mission of not getting lost in those smiles, she decided to say something, something that would not make her drift away again.
"So, what are you doing here?"
He looked taken back and blinked several times, a habit she knew of him whenever he was caught doing something.
He cleared his throat and answered.
"Er... I came to pick up some sanitary pads for my little sister, you know how you women can be" he chuckled and she smiled at it.
Her sisters would rather allow her to burn in shame of having her monthly period than help her get any pads or anything to ease her cramps.
"That is sweet of you, or are you sure it is not for one babe like that as you are using your sister as scope?" she jokingly asked.
"Cross my heart and hope to die" is his way of saying he was being truthful or making a promise.
"Oh, okay then..." she said not knowing what else to say.

"What... er... would you like to grab something to eat, like after the shopping?"
"How about your sister's pad, she would need them"
"She would need these ones for the rest of the week, she still has some to spare," he told her.
"Okay, okay yeah, I would like to," she said with a wide smile.
He smiled too and they kept looking at each other, nodding and letting out nervous chuckles before he broke it and looked away then looked back at her.
"We meet outside to get going?" he asked and she nods.
"Yeah, that is fine"
"Okay, see you in some hours or... maybe minutes," he said and she nods then they stood like that again, still looking at each other and giving each other goofy grins.
"Later," he said and she nods.
"Later" she replied and he walked away to get the pads while she watched him do that.
"Good LORD, he is gorgeous" she muttered under her breath as he picked a pad and looked at it before going ahead to pick out more.
He looked her way and she was startled that she got caught in 4k, she flashed him a nervous smile and went back to packing almost ten pads into the basket she carried and some other toiletries and deodorants.
When she had grabbed all that she needed, she looked up and he wasn't there so she went to the cashier to pay up.
It reaches her turned and her goods were packed.

"That would be twelve-thousand-naira ma"
"Okay, hold on" she opened her purse and brought out her card to pay but a hand stopped her and she looked at who was that to see Patrick nodding at the cashier who nods back and hands the already packed goods to her.
He told her to wait for him as he waited for his goods to be packed before paying with his card and walking out of the store with her.
"Thanks, but it wasn't necessary"
"Nah, I want to make a good impression, did I pass?" he popped a dimple to bribe her.
"Only because of your dimple so yes" he grinned.
"Did you bring your car? Mine is at the mechanic shop"
"Yeah, I parked over there" she pointed to a white BMW that was in between a truck and a corolla.
"Nice car I must say"
"Well, thank yo-" she cut herself off when she saw the very Tomiwa hand-in-hand with Beatrice her sister laughing and crossing to the other pedestrian walkway.
"Are you okay?" he asked when he saw her countenance change as she looked ahead to see the boyfriend of hers with one of her sisters laughing and being too close.
"What is he doing with her? And that close?"
She heaved a sigh and walked to the driver's seat and opened the door.

He looked at them then back at her before going to the passenger seat and closing the door as they stay in silence.
After a few moments, he spoke up.
"What is going on?"

That Trip

"That is a stupid and unmanly thing to do," he said after hearing all the explanations of her failed relationship.

"I know right?" she agreed and looked straight ahead with different thoughts going through her mind.

"I am sorry about this that happened to you, it is honestly his loss. I would be so happy to have someone like you or even you, in my life" he said.

"Someone is actually not shy at taking a shot" she chuckled and he grinned.

"I have never been shy about letting you know every single time," he told her with all honesty.

She smiled and looked away from him to get a side look of the window.

"I wouldn't lie, I liked you so much during college days and would just hide it because I thought that with Tomiwa it was different but I guess I was wrong" she let out a bitter laugh and lay her head on the steering wheel.

"Why did you hide what you felt for me?" he asked her and she lifts her head up to look at him.

"I loved Tomiwa, and the fact that my mum was easy on me when I brought home a man that hasn't lived abroad before as my boyfriend and how nice and tender she treated me" she frowned and could feel the tears build up in her eyes.

"I have never done something right in her eyes and it got worse when I applied to study business in Harvard and got accepted with a 50% paid scholarship all through my university years" a tear slipped down her cheek and he was quick to wipe them off before they trailed down to her chin.
"She kept saying I will get spoilt and I wouldn't have good values instilled in me if I go outside to study. Before, and after university, she kept comparing me with my sisters who schooled here in Nigeria and how culture-rich they are and how they wouldn't be like me" she closed her eyes and allowed the tears to fall.
"I was tagged as 'The girl who can't keep a relationship that isn't business' in my family but it subsided when I brought Tomiwa home. They said at least he could instill the right amount of values I needed to be a good wife and would even bad mouth me in front of him"
"That is sick"
She laughed.
"I know right? It was just so crazy and I think he was pressured into proposing to me too. I was supposed to do my master's programs overseas but they managed to convince him to make me do it here in Nigeria."
"I can't imagine what you are actually feeling as you are telling me all these. This is too much and no one deserves such treatment"
"They don't understand that" she cleaned her face and took out a wipe to blow her nose.

"Are you feeling better or do you still feel the need to cry more?" she chuckled and shook her head.
"No, I am fine, thank you so much for listening"
"It's fine, how are the twins? Dara and Dora, right?"
"Yes, those angels in disguise. They are good"
"Okay, since you are doing fine, let's go for that pre-dinner since it's almost five in the evening," he said checking his watch.
"Sure, fix in your seatbelt" she fixed hers and started the car.
"You pick wherever you want us to go"
"Okay then" she smiled and drove out of the parking lot to the road and to one of her favorite food spots in Lagos.
...
"You can't be serious" she exclaimed and took a sip from her drink as he tells her the story of what happened when he was babysitting his cousin.
"Omo, I was speechless and just in that shock phase where you can't react, move or do nothing because you are physically and mentally paralyzed by what you saw happening," he told her and she laughed then snorted and they both laughed at that.
"You just made me laugh and it was really so easy to flow with you"
"Could be because we have been close before" he said and she giggled.
"Thank you, Patrick"
"With all pleasure, what will you be doing?"
She paused in thought then something came to her.

"Will you be busy all through next week?" his brows furrowed as he looks at her.
"Er... no, why are you asking?"
"I have two tickets to Maldives for the whole of next week and need to bring someone with me as a friend" she explained to him and he felt his heart leap in the excitement that she was asking him.
"So you want me to be your plus one?"
"Yeah, if you'd come"
"I will when you buy me a pair of ballet shoes" he batted his eyes at her and she rolled her eyes.
"I am suspecting that as a yes"
"You got it girl" he winked and she shook her head before finishing her drink.
...
It was a bright Saturday morning and Patrick was sleeping peacefully at his home when suddenly he felt prickles of water on his face thereby interrupting his sleep.
He rubbed his face not wanting to wake at that moment then turned the other way and could feel the ray of light attack his eyes even though they were closed.
A groan of annoyance escaped his lips as he sat up with his eyes still closed and a frown gracing his face.
Slowly he opened his eyes to find the cause or the reason his sleep was disrupted.
When his eyes open a bit, it was met with the smiling face of a man who looked impressed that his aim was achieved.

He closed his eyes again and yawned as he stretched his limbs then rubbed his eyes before opening them again and this time wide enough to see the idiot in front of him.

"I was ready to throw this bucket of water all over you if you didn't have a plan of waking up or getting your butt off this bed" Yemi Ojo his neighbor/best friend said to him.

"And wet this bed with the blanket I cherish so much? I am hoping you don't have a death wish Yemi" Patrick said hoarsely then stretched again before getting up from the bed and heading for the bathroom with Yemi following behind.

"What? When that one wan start?" Patrick asked when his friend followed him to the bathroom.

"Wait, what are you thinking? I am just putting this bucket back where I saw it. I am too pretty for you abeg" he said and went to throw the water before putting the bucket on the floor and leaving the bathroom.

"What are you doing here? I thought you were still going to be with that girl who you told me stole your heart" Patrick asked then took a toothbrush to start brushing his teeth.

"Oh, that one? Mtcheew, abeg make we forget that one, she no worth am. This love thing na scam" Yemi said then sat on Patrick's bed.

"Love?" Patrick brought his head out of the bathroom to look at his friend who was sitting on his bed and looking at the ceiling.

"Why do you sound surprised?" Yemi asked with a frown directed at his friend who then let out a laugh.
"So, you sef don chop breakfast? Unbelievable" he finished brushing his teeth and washed his face then came out with a face towel that was around his neck and at the same time used it to clean his face.
"See guy this thing no funny at all. Like how babe go leave me? Me we most girls dey pray make I notice, she con leave me like that. Like say I no matter" he hissed and looked somewhere else.
"Ah! But I thought you don't want any relationship with any girls? You told me it was strictly 'do and move to the next' no strings attached, how come there were strings attached to this one?"
"Me I no understand oo, like how that one take happen? I no even touch the girl sef and she con do me like this" Yemi lamented bitterly and shook his head.
"I told you that this your pompous nature will come and bite you in the butt one day but you told me that you don't have a heart to love any woman, that they were just there to warm your bed"
"I know but I don't understand how Sarah take hold me like this, like me, a whole me. Yemi the ladies man, the one that gets any lady with a wink don chop breakfast, chai"
"But let us talk seriously, you like this girl?"
"I do, a lot"
"Why then did she leave you?" Patrick asked.
"I wanted to be real with her when I realize I was catching feelings already and planned on telling her all

about my past after we go on a trip I planned for us both"
"She left because of that?"
"Not really, it was because she heard it from someone else and she became angry and thought I wanted to use her then dump her so that was why she left"
Patrick sighed and thought about it for a while before speaking up.
"Have you tried talking to her? Reaching out to her?"
"I called her once but she didn't pick up"
"Once? Guy you are not ready yet, babe wey you love you wan leave am like that? Instead of you to go and beg her and explain to her, find all means you can to explain things to her and if she chooses to stick with you then fine, if not you will find that right girl"
"No, I want Sarah, if it is not her then I don't want another person"
"Good luck to you friend. You know that valentine is coming soon so you better get your legs walking to her house to get her, if not you will chop lunch and dinner join"
"Abeg shut up, how about you? Who will you be spending this valentine with? Is it Angela? I don't like that girl. Her shakara is too much"
"No, not Angela and I have to continue my packing sef... I was so tired when I came home from work yesterday" Patrick stood up to bring out his half-packed suitcase from his closet.
"Packing? To where?"
"You remember Ife?" Patrick turned to look at his friend who had a confused look on his face.

"Ifeoluwa Tobiloba, my crush from college" he reminded him.

A look of surprise and amusement filled Yemi's face as he recalled her.

"That babe wey you dey fall for over and over again, even when she pick one local man over you? How she be? Is she still as curvy as she was in college?" Yemi wriggled his brows and earned a glare from Patrick.

"You fool, so you were looking at her like that?"

"Guy chill, I no want your babe, she isn't my type. I am a man and when I see a watermelon, I can't call it a mango" he defends himself.

"Abeg shut up, she is fine, thanks for asking and we are going to Maldives for the whole of valentine's week" he explained and went back to packing.

"Ehn ehn, just like that? How did you both meet again? Or have you been secretly dating her before now?"

"No, we met some days ago and she is more beautiful than I remember" he stopped packing and stood as he remembers how she looked when he saw her in the store.

"Beautiful, she wore baggy clothes so I couldn't see her curves but I am sure she still has them. Chai, GOD really took his time to make her because she is one of his best masterpieces, fine geh"

"Hmm, so you still love that girl? And it has been how many years now? Three... two years?"

"Who wouldn't? She is kindhearted, beautiful, has a great sense of humor, and a really good person" he shrugged and pack the last of the clothes he was taking along with him.

"I would agree on that with you, so it will be the romantic one you have always dreamed about going to with her?" Yemi wriggled his brows again.

"No, not really. I have always dreamed of taking her to Maldives for a romantic getaway but this time, she is healing from a painful heartbreak and I am going with her as a friend"

"You want to be friend-zoned again? Remember college days?"

"I wasn't friend-zoned, I agree I do tell her all the time that I like her and she would always tell me that she sees me more as a friend and I understand and respect her choice, even though I wished she would have romantic feelings towards me in the future"

"Do you think she likes you as you wanted?" Yemi asked with furrowed brows.

"As I said, she is nursing a broken heart so I can't say or push anything on her. I want her to heal independently so she can then decide if she wants me or not"

"Anyhow sha, don't let someone play with your feelings all in the name of wanting a shoulder to cry on" Yemi warned.

"Ife isn't like that" Patrick defended.

"Whatever you say, when do you leave?"

"Tomorrow after church, 4 pm"

"I wish you a safe journey and you both should enjoy yourselves. I will go and meet my babe so you can get on with your preparations. My regards to Ifeoluwa"

Yemi stood up the stretched before making his way to the door.
"Sure, go get her and my regards to Sarah"
"Bye"

***

Translations

Mtcheew - is a hissing sound.
Abeg make we forget that one, she no worth am. This love thing na scam - Please let us forget about her, she isn't worth it. this love thing is a scam.
So, you sef don chop breakfast? - You too got your heart broken?
See guy this thing no funny at all. Like how babe go leave me? Me we most girls dey pray make I notice, she con leave me like that. Like say I no matter - See guy this thing isn't funny at all. Like how will a girl leave me? When most girls are praying that I notice them, she left me. Like I don't matter.
Me I no understand oo, like how that one take happen? I no even touch the girl sef and she con do me like this - Even I don't understand, like how did it happen? I wasn't even intimate with her and she treated me like this.
I know but I don't understand how Sarah take hold me like this, like me, a whole me. Yemi the ladies man, the one that gets any lady with a wink don chop breakfast, chai - I know but i don't understand how Sarah got me where no one has, like me the ladies

man, the one that gets any lady with a wink got his heart broken.

Babe wey you love you wan leave am like that? - You want to leave a girl you love just like that?

If not you will chop lunch and dinner join - You wouldn't be able to handle the next heartbreak that would follow.

Shakara in this case means playing hard to get.

That babe wey you dey fall for over and over again, even when she pick one local man over you? - That girl that you fell in love with and pick another guy over you?

Guy chill, I no want your babe - Bro, be calm, I don't want your girl.

Maldives 1

Day 1 - Sunday 8th February 2022

"Amen" everyone chorused in the church as the pastor said words of prayer to the congregation.
"This week will be good for you in JESUS name"
"Amen!" a woman stood up with her hands up in the air as she screamed the loudest amen with all her might.
"Shout a big, big amen"
"Amen!"
"If you know that this week is your week, stand up and shout the loudest amen"
Everyone in the church stood up and screamed Amen! Some even stood in their chair.
"You may all have your seat," and everyone sat back down as he continued with the preaching.
Soon after the pastor was through with the sermon and welcomed the dance group of the church as they came to perform.
□ Valentine is coming...
Where is your boyfriend?
Valentine is coming...
Where is your girlfriend?
Valentine is coming...
All you need is JESUS □

They all continued to sing and dance to the song for almost thirty minutes before leaving when they were through.

Is that what they should be singing today?

She asked herself as she shook her head at them then some children from the children's church department came to sing some lovely songs they were taught by their teachers which was so impressive.

The service had ended some minutes ago after the numerous activities and the final proclamation of blessings from the senior pastor.

Ifeoluwa made her way out of the auditorium after greeting some of the elders, members, and workers she came across then made her way to her car.

Just as she unlocked her car with her keys and was about to open the door to get in, a voice called from behind her and she turned to see who the voice belonged to.

One of the men from the dance group who goes by the name David walked up to her with a large smile on his face and she returned the smile also.

"Ife mi, bawo ni?" he asked.

Ifeoluwa rolled her eyes and shook her head then replied to him.

"I am not your Ife, I have told you that countless times"

"Eh, anyhow sha. Will y-"

"Ah! Ope oo, Ife decided to show up in church today" a lady who goes by the name Funmilayo said as she approaches them.

An annoyed look suddenly graced Ife's face as she looked at Funmi.

"Funmi, what is the meaning of that? I don't like it oo. You are making it look like I don't go to church or listen to sermons at all"

Funmi let out a laugh.

"Person wey no dey go church like that, na him dey sin pass" she lets out another laugh.

Ife gave her a disapproving look and a shake of her head.

"And you call yourself a Christian without knowing the true meaning of Christianity"

"If you are aware of what 'Christianity' is all about, why don't you enlighten me madam 'i know only business'" Funmi said and a flash of disappointment went through Ife's eyes.

"I don't know too much about Christianity either but I am aware that GOD uses our hearts and conscience to judge us. He isn't like we humans that use the outer part of a person to judge who they really are" she explained and Funmi glared at her.

"If you are really a Christian you should actually start doing what GOD wants you to do and stop doing his work for him. He didn't ask for your help and he would never need it"

"So your point?"

"My point is you should start seeing things the way GOD sees things and don't use someone lack of not attending physical services to judge whether they are Christians, sinners or whatsoever," Ife told her.

"A little advice, stop judging people. Your level of Christianity might quicken if you try such exercise"

"Whatever, madam advisor. Are you coming for the service that would be held in the church on Val's day?"

"I was going to ask," David said looking at Ife for her answer.

"No,"

"Why? I thought you and Tomiwa already broke up?"

"Sister Funmi, that is not how to talk to someone nau even though you heard a rumor" David cautioned her and she ignored him then looked at Ife for an answer.

"Yes, things didn't work out well but I thank GOD we had not gotten married yet before he decided to make this rash decision" Ife put a smile on her face as she answered her.

She didn't feel too heartbroken about it anymore and was gradually healing from it.

"If you are not going to Maldives with Tomiwa, who is now coming with you?"

"That is none of your business, I will catch you guys later. Bye" she said and entered her car then immediately started the engine and drove out of the church compound.

...

"I just wonder what her business was with your life," Dara said helping Ife pack the last of her luggage for her one-week trip.

"She isn't the important thing at the moment, what is important is that I still get to spend this holiday with

someone I want to bond with and in a friendly manner," Ife said and shrugged.
"Who knows, it could be something else" Dora wriggled her brows, and Ife rolled her eyes.
"Think whatever you want to think but this is going to stay on neutral ground and nothing else. At least we get to have a friendly valentine's week" she shrugs again and both twins exchange knowing looks.
"Anyhow, sha be gisting us of anything, okay?"
"I have heard you, I should get going so I will not miss my flight. Thank you, girls, I love you both so much" she hugged them both and they chuckled.
"What will you do without us?" Dora asked.
"You don't need to keep thanking us. That is what family is for" Dara told her and she smiled then let go of the hug.
"I am really going to be missing you girls, take care okay? And call me if anything is up" she made her way downstairs and to the door with the twins following behind carrying her bags for her.
"Sure, enjoy yourselves" Dara winked and Ife threw her a playful glare.
They went out of the house to the taxi that was waiting for her outside the apartment building.
After she had entered and they put her bags in the boot of the car, they waved at her as the taxi drove off.
"Let this be a new beginning of joy and forever happiness for her" Dara said as they watched the taxi go far till it turned a corner.

"Amen, we should toast to that" Dora replied and they headed inside.

...

"Hi," she said from behind him and he turned to look at her with a smile automatically displaying on his lips. She was glad they had gotten there on time, with the traffic they faced on their way to the airport.

When she reached the airport she took a cab to the departure gate then when she reached, she went to the departure lounge and searched around for him because he had texted her that he was already at the departure lounge.

"I thought you were going to bail on me" he joked and she laughed then came to sit beside him.

"Would not be able to handle that heartbreak too" she joked back and he grinned.

"So how was service today?"

"Great, it was as if the pastor knew I was traveling because of the amount of prayer her rained on us in service today"

"Not the usual kind?"

"Not the usual kind" she confirmed.

"How was service today?"

"Great, I watched it online though"

"That is great. Connecting to the most high wherever you maybe is important"

"Over important sef" he agreed and she nodded.

They continued talking for a while before the announcer told them they could start boarding the plane.

After they had entered and buckled up when the air hostess had displayed all the safety measures to take in case there is an emergency.

"This is it" she turned to him to say and he smiled and nod his head.

"This is it," he said after her.

"See you in Maldives"

"And you to madam," he said in an accent she couldn't recognize.

***

Translations

Ife mi, bawo ni? - My love, how are you?

Ife is Love

Ope oo - Thank GOD oo.

Person wey no dey go church like that, na him dey sin pass - Someone that hardly ever goes to church sins the most.

Maldives 2

Day 2 - Monday 9th February 2022

The sun shined so brightly and laying on the king-sized white bed spread is Ife, with the blanket covering her small frame as she stretched and moved her body on the wide space.

They arrived in Maldives in the night. They both talked, gist, laughed, and got to know more about each other while on the plane.

When they had gotten there, they were tired and were thankful that they saw a taxi that took them straight to the hotel they were going to be staying at.

It was a double bedroom ensuite that when you look from the floor to ceiling windows, the swimming pool and resort area could be seen.

It was beautiful and she didn't have the strength to dwell in the beauty of the place because of how tired she was from the flight and just retired to bed.

He was thinking she might have known that the room she picked was larger than his and just used 'being tired' to get it first but he was fine, just so far she was okay and comfortable.

He had woken up early to order a breakfast buffet for them both.

He made sure there was enough wheat bread and mayonnaise. He knows it to be her favorite food any time of the day.

Hopefully, it is still her favorite.

After taking a bath, getting dressed in a light blue Hawaiian shirt that had the top three buttons opened, brown khaki shorts, and a pair of flip flops.

It was already almost eleven in the morning and she was still sleeping so he decided to go into her room that wasn't locked after some minutes of knocking with no response.

When he got in, the window was slightly opened, his eyes went to her sleeping figure on the bed and saw her sleeping in a weird position.

He chuckled and went ahead to open the window and it illuminated the whole room.

Small groans and moving were heard coming from the bed and he turned to look at her before walking up to her.

"Rise and shine beauty" he leaned down to whisper to her and she opened her eyes to look at him before closing them back, yawning and stretching at the same time.

"Good morning" she greets him hoarsely and yawned again.

He chuckled again and sat on the bed while still looking down at her.

"Good morning to you too" he replied "Did you sleep well?"

"Very, this bed is comfy and large" she spread her hands and legs as she explains the comfort she felt laying on the bed.

"It's good to know but as good and soft it might be, you need to get up so we can do some activities today and not just lay down on the bed all day," he told her and she sat up to face him as she nods in agreement.

"Yeah, we didn't fly all the way to just lay on the bed and do nothing. She got up from the bed and stretched yet again before heading for the bathroom to brush her teeth and wash her face.

By the time she came out of the bathroom, her eyes were presented by a big table full of buffet.

From croissant to potato pudding to a medium-sized mayonnaise to a loaf of wheat bread which made her eyes lit up like she got what she had requested for Christmas.

There were some juice, yogurt, pancakes with syrup bottles, scrambled eggs, cereal, and a lot more that made her stomach grumble the more at the mere sight.

Her mouth hung open as she made her way to the bed still looking at the table. She really hoped she wasn't drooling or sort but the sight of all these tantalizing breakfast buffets made that the least of her worries.

"You like?" Patrick asked, looking at how mesmerized she was when her eyes met with the buffet.

She nods and mutters something that he couldn't pick point.

"Well, come sit and enjoy these wonderfully made breakfasts," he told her and she came to sit beside him while he put an empty plate in front of her and started with the wheat bread and opened the mayonnaise so she could scoop as much as she wanted.

"You know my favorite food." she cooed as she looked at him in admiration.

"I wouldn't consider this food but I always kept what you liked and most things I know about you here in my heart," he told her and she could feel her head flutter at what he said.

'Did he really mean what he was saying?' she asked herself as she kept looking at him and how he put the amount of scrambled eggs she likes besides the bread before handing her a spoon to scoop the mayonnaise.

"That is so sweet of you Patrick," she said after a while of staring.

He smiled with his dimples showing which made her blush and look away.

"Enjoy your meal girl" he patted her arm and dishes out his food too.

They began eating and talking about so many things, what they had been up to all those times they weren't in contact with each other and so many more things.

They were almost done with most of the food on the table and were already getting full with what they had consumed.

"To a great vacation" Ife took the yogurt she was holding and held it out to him.

He held out the ice tea he was drinking and clicked it with hers.

"To a memorable one filled with joy, healing, and laughter" he winked and drank his tea while she took a spoon from her yogurt before placing it on the table.

"I am almost full so I will stop here so we can get on with today's activities except you just want us to stay in."

"No Ife, we are going out and it would be somewhere fun, so go get ready while I get the room service to come to get this table. Wear something simple" he told her and left to his room with the table.

"Something simple on its way," she said and went in to go and get ready.

...

She laughed so hard at what he whispered in her ear then pushed him playfully as they walked their way back to the hotel.

She had wanted them to go by cab back to the hotel but he suggested that they just have a cool evening walk which she thought was a good idea.

"Patrick you are just as funny, fun to be with, amazing, cheeky, and a very gorgeous human like you have always been but just better," she told him and he felt his heart warm at what she said.

"Now it's getting to my head" he responded and she giggled.

"Don't let it" she playfully warned and they continued walking in silence.

"I really had fun today Patrick, thank you for being here with me and making me feel good" she glanced at him and he flashed her a smile.
"Nah, it's fine. What are friends for?" he asked and she looked at him then nod her head before looking away.
She didn't know what she was expecting him to say but him saying that eased down some kind of softness that gradually developed as they went to different places to have the time of their lives.
She wanted to bring someone here with her on a friendly vacation with the hope that the person wouldn't catch any feelings but with how she is feeling for this fine man, she doubts it wouldn't be them catching feelings.
'The LORD help my soul' she prayed within.
They got to the hotel in no time, then retired for their respective rooms to rest for the night and get ready for what the next day brings for them.

Day 3 - Tuesday 10th February 2022

They got up quite late and after talking and talking and talking for hours they realized how hungry they were and decided to eat out for that morning.
He had googled some cool breakfast spot they could have brunch since it was already some minutes past twelve in the afternoon.
After having brunch, they sat there for a while to relax before getting up and walking down the street at

the same time window shopping and taking photos of each other.

He informed her of a park he noticed on the map as he looked through for the spot they had brunch at and she agreed for them to go there.

On their way there, a particular necklace caught her eyes and she dragged him with her to go into the local shop that had it displayed to ask for a price.

She was amazed to have seen another necklace that is of the same color and design with just a slight difference in the sizes but they were exactly alike.

Dara and Dora came into her mind and she purchased them immediately and had them wrapped so that once she lands in Nigeria and sees them, she would just hand them over to each of them.

"Those girls would be glad you had them in mind," he said when they had purchased the necklace and were headed for the park again.

"I always have them in mind, I just hope they love it and since it came as a twin, why not gift them to my twin friends?" she responded with a chuckle.

"I am sure they would," he told her and put his arms around her shoulder.

When they got there, they looked for a spot to stay and concluded under the tree was okay for them to stay.

"Sorry, we didn't pack a picnic basket to have another date," he told her and she raised a brow at what he said.

"A date?" she asked and he froze then looked at her with eyes wide open and heart beating so fast as he searched his head for what to reply to her.

"Er... yeah? Fri-"

"A date," she said again and smiled with a nod "a date it is," she said and saw him visibly relax.

"You don't mind?"

"Not at all, forget the basket, we can do another time that would have the basket involved," she told him and he grinned widely.

"Well no problem dear, you are going to love this date"

"Yesterday friendly outing was amazing so I trust your words"

He smiled and they started talking about each other, asking more questions, likes, dislikes, favorite food, things to do, sport, etc.

In the middle of their talk, a woman and her daughter, holding two baskets that were covered with a small blanket walked over to them to sell the basket they had with them.

They said they had noticed that they had come here and would have forgotten their picnic basket so they wanted to sell it for them and at a discounted price since valentine was at the corner.

There were a variety of foods, snacks, and drinks in there with a folded note that read 'To a lovely couple, many more years in love and happiness! Cheers'

Ifeoluwa was thrilled and Patrick couldn't hide the smile that stuck to his face when they read the note.

They had fun, chatted for a while and when it got darker they decided to head back to the hotel and call it a day.

Maldives 3

Day 4/5 - Wednesday 11th/ Thursday 12th February 2022

They didn't do much on their fourth and fifth day aside from staying indoors and doing a movie marathon that each of them picked to watch.

They talked some more in between the movies and realized with all the times they spent together and talked, they had some things in common and were liking each other all over again.

She had wanted to keep it all on a platonic level but she feels like this wouldn't last long and it might be like the last time she thought she had the hots for him and would then run away or hide just so the feelings can pass.

Whichever it would be, she hopes it is for the best.

Day 6 - Friday 13th February 2022

It was the eves of Valentine and they both agreed on going to the beach to relax and on their way check out for a restaurant they could dine at later in the evening.

"Or we could go shopping instead?" Patrick asked when a thought went through his mind for what they could do instead.

"Shopping?" she asked then after wearing the second leg of her white sneaker then stood up to go get her earrings on the dresser table.

"Yeah, shopping. Like we could find some things to take home for the girls and my buddy Yemi" he told her and she chuckled.

"You are still friends with Yemi?" she asked and he came to stand behind her as they looked into each other's eyes from the mirror.

"Yeah, forgetting the part where he is the main ladies man, he is a great friend and has an amazing personality" he defends his friend.

"No need to get all defensive. I was just... you know curious and I am aware for a fact that Yemi is an amazing person. If you would ignore his ashawo behavior, you will see a caring and kind-hearted person in there"

"You seem to have had an encounter with him and I am very sure I am not aware of this encounter," he told her and she turned to look at him with a smile on her face.

"Do I sense jealousy?"

"Well, it could be but I wouldn't be jealous of him because number one... " he held out his index finger "he is my best friend, number two..." he held out his thumb "he is already hooked to a girl he sees and wants only so there wouldn't be any need for that jealousy shit" he raised a brow and made sure his dimples were showing.

"I feel like I am going to fall for you if you keep showing me how cute your dimples look on you," she told him and he laughed.

"Well, fall baby because I had fallen for a very long time" he made his voice so deep as he said those words to her.

Her heart skipped, her hands shook, her legs felt weak and her eyes wanted to roll to the back of her head by just hearing his voice sound like that.

He was doing things to her and if she wasn't careful, she would fall as he asked her to.

Placing her hands on the table behind her to hold up her weight as she felt like her legs would give up on her and make her fall, she leaned back and breathed through her mouth to calm down her senses.

"Are you okay?" he moved a step towards her when he saw her take in a deep breath through her mouth.

She stopped him by putting her hands out to him and breathing in and out constantly till she was calm. When she felt like she was calm, she stood on her feet and walked away from the dresser to the bed so she could pick up the small bag they were carrying to the beach.

"Let's go?" she asked and he nodded his head then followed her from behind.

On their way to the beach, Patrick had been on the phone with someone who he had been talking to about plans, what they would like, him coming to check them out or they sending the pictures so he could select his preferred choice.

It kind of irritated her that he didn't get off the phone till they got to the beach and settled on one of the lounges.

He got out of the phone and apologize for the long phone call which she didn't feel the need to get angry at him for. It could be something he wanted to have fixed up and she shouldn't push herself to him or make him see her as needy.

They stayed on the beach for almost an hour and he reminded her about their shopping before they packed up and went to get some cocktails at the bar before leaving the beach finally.

He excused himself to take another call and she didn't do anything to hide her irritation but didn't let him see how irritated she was and just looked away when he said he wanted to take the call.

She drank from her cup slowly and looked at the beach which wasn't that far from the bar. She could see everyone having great times with their families, some were lovers holding hands, staring out the beach, leaving kisses on each other skin and lips, running after each other.

A sigh left her lips as she looked away from them. this had been her initial plans with Tomiwa but he ruined them all. She went from being engaged to being single in just a snap of a finger and it made her heart heavy and she suddenly felt the need to cry.

"Everything okay beautiful?" she heard someone say from behind her and she turned around to meet with very bright ocean blue eyes, blond hair, shirtless toned abs, fine biceps, swim shorts hanging on his waist, and a cute smile.

She had to turn to look at him properly and her heart leaped at the gorgeous creation of GOD that was now standing behind her.

'Chai, see fine boy' she said in her mind as she kept assessing him.

A deep chuckle left his lips and that brought her out of the faze she found herself in.

"You like what you see?" he bit his bottom lip and leaned on the counter as he checked her out.

"Uh..." it felt like her head was at a loss of words as she tried to think of what to say to him so it wouldn't give him the wrong idea.

He was gorgeous and all but was not her type, she was just taken aback when she was met with his beautiful appearance.

"Babe, are you ready?" she heard Patrick say from behind her and she turned to look at him with her eyes slightly going wider than usual before returning to their normal size.

"Oh, you have a boyfriend?" the handsome stranger said and she turned to him and just stared.

She was in the midst of two gorgeous looking men and that alone was mind-blowing, astounding, breathtaking, wonderful, ex-

"I would leave you two, bye beautiful," the stranger said taking her out of the little bubble she floated in and walking away but she didn't miss the wink he threw her way.

"Were you bored?" he asked when he sat down to finish up his drink.

"Uh?" she asked still recovering from that encounter.

"Nevermind, let us go" he held her hand and they walked away from the bar and out of the beach.

...

"Do you think they would like this?" she asked but got no response so she turned around to see that he wasn't anywhere around.

"But he was just here some minutes ago?" she asked herself out loud then put the cloth she held on her arm back at where she took it from and walked along the aisle they were shopping at.

'Where could he have gone to?' she wondered and kept looking around then she turned to the toiletries aisle and checked but couldn't see him there too.

Taking her phone out of her pocket, she went to the call app and dialed his number, but she stopped as she was about to press the call button.

"Thank you so much" she heard a familiar voice say and had to walk to the aisle next to the toiletries to confirm her suspicion.

Her eyes widened in shock, her heart became heavy and she could feel the tears gather in her eyes as she saw them.

Patrick had his arms around a woman and the woman's arms were around his. It wasn't the 'we're just meeting for the first-time kind of hug'.

It looked like they had known for ages and were meeting after a long time as they shared what she considers to be an intimate hug.

Reasons she felt betrayed was unknown to her but she didn't like what she just saw and then it occurred to her that she might be the one he had been talking to all the while they were on their way to the beach when they were about coming here and while they were still here.

"He even had the guts to ditch me there to come to meet up with her" she muttered and felt so sad.

This holiday was supposed to make her heal and bring her calmness since she was going with her long-time friend but she is feeling the total opposite now and just wants to be away from him.

She went back to the aisle to continue the shopping but wasn't feeling it so she decided to head for the bathroom to calm herself down.

On her way there she stumbled upon Patrick who was holding a dress in his hand and wanted to ask him about that lady. She thought she might seem pushy if she start asking questions like she was his girlfriend or so.

Asking him where he went would be okay and friendly-wise so she cleared her throat and opened her mouth to speak but he beats her to it.

"Where are you going? Are you done shopping?" he asked and she blinked then shook her head 'no'.

"Where were you?" she blurted out and ignored his question.

His brows furrowed before they relaxed then he looked around and allowed a chuckle to leave his lips.

"I was getting a dress" he replied.

"With who?" she didn't know when she asked and had to clear her throat to cover it up when he frowned at that.
"I-i-- I will be back soon" she brushed past him and went to the bathroom quickly before her legs failed her.

Day 7 - Saturday 14th February 2022

Patrick had been quite worried about Ife's sudden disappearance. He had tried her phone countless time but it wasn't going through till the last time it said switched off.
He noticed her strange behavior when he came back from meeting with Anna his long-time friend who lives here. They were planning something huge and he didn't want Ife to have any idea about it that was why he was being discreet about it.
When they had come back from the shopping which was quite early mainly because Ife said she was tired and wanted to rest he didn't object and wanted her to have enough rest for the activities of today which is valentines day.
She was quiet all the way here and would answer in monophthongs when he asked her something or would try to spike up a conversation. When they had reached, she went straight to her room without saying anything, not even goodbye or that heartwarming smile she gives him every time.
He wondered what could have been the problem and what could have made her mood go sour in just

minutes that he left and came back. It was like she ate bad food or didn't get what she requested for Christmas and it made him worried but hoped that today would cheer her up.

"Could this be something about her ex? Did she feel lonely because valentine is here and she doesn't get to spend it with the man she loved?" he asked himself out loud and felt his heart go heavy from that thought.

He really wished she would forget about that man and concentrate on him who would help her heal from this heartbreak and not cause her to be sad.

Switching his phone back on, he dialed Anna's number and explained his predicament to her.

...

"What are you doing here sitting alone?" she heard a voice say from behind her and got startled a bit then calmed down when she turned to see who it was.

"Mystery man from yesterday," she said and looked straight ahead at the beach.

A chuckled revibrated from his lips and he came to sit beside her on the bench but not too close.

"You forgot to add handsome," he said and she let out a laugh.

"Proud much?"

"Who wouldn't be?" he asked back and she shook her head and sighed.

"It is Valentine's day and you didn't come here today with your boyfriend but here you are sitting all alone and looking at the beach for almost the whole day. Does he know you are here?" he asked.

"Nah, how about you. Why aren't you here with your girlfriend or something?" she asked and he smiled at her.

"Well, one, I own the bar there," he pointed behind them and she gave him an impressed look. "Two, she would have been here but I lost her to an auto accident last month," he told her and the smile went off her face in seconds.

"Oh my GOD, I am so sorry to hear that. I didn't mean to br-"

"It's fine though, you didn't know so..." he shrugged and looked away for a moment before looking back at her face that had sympathy written on it.

"We were expecting and I didn't know till the crash so... let's not talk about that, we should be merry, it's the season of love and we shouldn't be sad," he said to her and flashed her a smile.

She just stared at him and wondered why she was feeling sad in the first place. Tomiwa was her least concern now and even though Patrick had some other girl he was going out with at least he came here with her and put smiles upon smiles on her face and that was more than enough.

"You are very strong for this and I hope GOD gives you the strength you need to heal properly"

"I hope so too" he replied and she stood up to leave.

"Thank you for keeping me company but I would like to head back"

"Sure, just let him know not to hurt you again"

"He didn't hurt me"

"Whatever you say and enjoy your valentine evening" she nods and left the beach so she could head back.

When she switched on her phone it was like a time bomb of messages was set for when her phone comes on as messages upon messages started kicking in.

Most of them came from Patrick (including calls), Dara, her mum, and someone she never expected to get any calls from. Tomiwa.

Her heart felt heavy and she felt confused about whether or not to read his message or not. After contemplating for some minutes, she was going to tap on his message when a new one came from Patrick and she had already tapped it.

There were many messages from him and she frowned at the number of messages she was seeing. She scrolled up to check where it started from when a call from him came in and she looked at her screen then asked herself if she should pick it up or not.

She had gone out for a very long time without telling him anything and even switched off her phone to avoid calls from anyone so when she picks she would have to explain where she was, why she left without telling him about her whereabouts, why she wasn't picking her calls and what the matter was.

Explaining anything to anybody was the last thing she wanted to do at this time so she shook her head and ignored it so she could get back in time and hopefully sneak into her room without him noticing.

Maldives 4

"Where have you been?" she jumped when a voice said at a corner of the slightly dark room.

She turned to the source of the voice and placed her hand on her chest to even her fast-beating heart.

"Oh my GOD Patrick, you scared me," she said and let out a small chuckle.

He came out of the shadows with his arms crossed and was wearing blue jean trousers, a white button-up shirt that was rolled up to his elbow coupled with black leather fashion shoe. He looked great and she couldn't deny that.

"Where have you been?" he asked again and she saw annoyance mixed with worry on his face as he stares at her.

"I... uh... I went somewhere?" she asked and he narrowed his gaze at her and moved a step closer to her to which she took one back.

"Somewhere where?" he asked raising his eyebrows this time.

"Why do you care?" she blurts out in irritation.

He let out a humorous chuckle and looked around before settling his gaze on her.

"Why do I care? Ifeoluwa Tobiloba, you went out since morning without telling me or trying to drop a message about your whereabouts and when you will be back or keeping me updated so I wouldn't be so worried and aimlessly looking around for you and you have the guts to ask 'why do I care?' that is ridiculous" he said with disappointment.

She felt bad that she made him so worried and didn't bother to answer his call when he called but what she found out the previous day didn't allow her to see what she did and just didn't want to talk to him or anything.

He was dressed like he was heading out for a nice romantic dinner or just came back from one who knows and might just be playing the 'I care' card so that she thinks that he cares when he doesn't.

'I am not falling for that' she said in her mind.

"I am sorry that I made you worried even though you might be lying about that" she walked past him and went to settle on her bed to take off her shoes.

"Excuse me what made you think about that?" he asked as confusion played on his face.

"Oh please don't play 'I don't know what you are saying with me' you are very much aware of what I am saying and I would like to be left alone so please leave," she said and lay on her bed but he didn't leave.

"What happened? Why are you acting in this manner? I saw how your countenance changed when I came to meet with you after taking that call and you were not the smiling and cheerful Ife that I knew. What is the matter? Is it something that I did?" he asked and that angered her the more.

She sat up and looked at him with tears in her eyes and an angry look.

"You are asking me what you did wrong? I just don't understand you, men, it's like you all are just the same. You just can't stay with one woman and be happy, I don't understand" she lashed out at him and stood up from the bed.

He was taken aback by her sudden act and accusing words directed at him then it made him wonder what exactly he did wrong and why was she talking like that?"

"I really want to know what I might have done to deserve this sudden outburst from you," he said calmly and she turned to give him a glare then took in a deep breath let it out before talking.

"Yesterday, at the mall. You left me because you wanted to meet up with a woman even after telling me all those lies that you like me and all. I can't believe you, Patrick, I honestly can't" she shook her head at him in disgust and walked away from him to the opened window.

He visibly calm down and smiled when she said that before walking up to her.

"So that is what got you all worked up?" he asked and she turned to look at him, surprised at how cool he sounded with the allegations she laid against him.

"What are you smiling for?" she asked in anger.

"If that was what made you all worked up, you should be calming down," he told her and held her wrist then walked in the direction of his room with her following along.

"Leave me alone, I don't want to go anywhere with you"

"Be calm jare" he said to her and opened his room and walked them in.

"See, I don't have the ti-" she was interrupted when he switched on a few lights in the room that was bright enough to show a really romantic dinner setting.

There were two chairs sitting in the middle of the room, with red petals scattered on the floor, two big heart-shaped balloons were tied to a small table that says *'Happy Valentines to an Incredible Woman'*.

Small scented candles lay on the floor around the chairs to form a love shape and when she turned to look at him, he was holding out a rose to her.

She could feel her eyes water at what she saw and was speechless.

He could feel the satisfaction go through his system when he saw the look on her face and was impressed that he was able to pull off something like this and make her feel great.

That was what he thought but he needed her to tell him her thoughts on it so he wouldn't just base his assumptions on how she looked at the moment.

"How do you like it?" he asked and she burst out crying then went in his embrace to continue sobbing.

He rubbed her back to give her comfort and rocked them side to side till she calmed down.

"I really want to know how you feel toward this because I am so nervous abo-" he stopped when she kissed his cheek and felt them warm up from that little gesture of her.

"I love it, thank you," she said still hugging him and he let out a sigh of relief and carried her then twirl her around before putting her back to the floor.
"This was the reason for the phone calls and all the suspense, I have always wanted to have a great vacation with you here in the Maldives so when you invited me I was happy and also wanted to make this something you will forever remember," he told her when they leaned back from the hug.
"I will for sure remember this day," she told him and clean her face "Sorry for all the drama I put on"
"It's fine, I understand women and how they tend to act on certain things, especially when it isn't what they expect" he walked them both to the table and held out the chair for her to sit before going to bring the food table they could take whatever they wanted from.
"I would have booked us a private chef or waiter here but I guess you might need the privacy," he told her and sat in front of her.
"I am glad you didn't," she said then poured them both wines in their cups.
"Happy Valentine's day Ifeoluwa"
"Happy Valentine's day Patrick" they clicked their glasses and started eating.

About the Author

Bethel-Gold

Bethel-Gold officially started writing since 2021. She writes Clean romance, Christian romance, YA/Teen fiction and when she isn't writing, she is designing, reading books of her favorite authors or creating crafty works that involves accessories, ornaments etc.

www.ingramcontent.com/pod-product-compliance
Lightning Source LLC
LaVergne TN
LVHW091230150826
845673LV00003B/1079

* 9 7 8 9 3 5 6 4 5 0 2 3 3 *